MAMMOTH

SIMON & SCHUSTER

First published in Great Britain in 2021 by Simon & Schuster UK Ltd, 1st Floor,
222 Gray's Inn Road, London, WC1X 8HB · Text copyright © 2021 Anna Kemp
Illustrations copyright © 2021 Adam Beer · The right of Anna Kemp and
Adam Beer to be identified as the author and illustrator of this work has been
asserted by them in accordance with the Copyright, Designs and Patents Act,
1988 · All rights reserved, including the right of reproduction in whole or in
part in any form · A CIP catalogue record for this book is available from the
British Library upon request · 978-1-4711-9159-6 (HB) · 978-1-4711-9158-9
(PB) · 978-1-4711-9157-2 (eBook)
Printed in Great Britain by Bell and Bain Ltd, Glasgow · 10 9 8 7 6 5 4 3 2

MAMMOTH

Anna Kemp and Adam Beer

SIMON & SCHUSTER

London   New York   Sydney   Toronto   New Delhi

The mammoth had no idea how long he had been asleep, but he was very cold and very hungry.

So he shook the ice from his fur and went to the meadow to join his herd for breakfast.

But his herd wasn't there . . .

Just some giant, shiny beetles, crawling in circles and making a horrible din.

The mammoth blinked and looked about him.

Strange creatures in the meadow;
strange birds in the sky.

He'd never known a stranger morning.

He climbed to the top of the hill to get a better look.

Where was his herd? Was this a joke?
The mammoth frowned. It wasn't very funny.

Then, far off in the distance, he saw a huge, gleaming forest.
The mammoth scratched his woolly head.

Where had that come from?

He made his way towards the great, shining trees,

trumpeting for his cousins and his aunties.

But only the beetles trumpeted back.

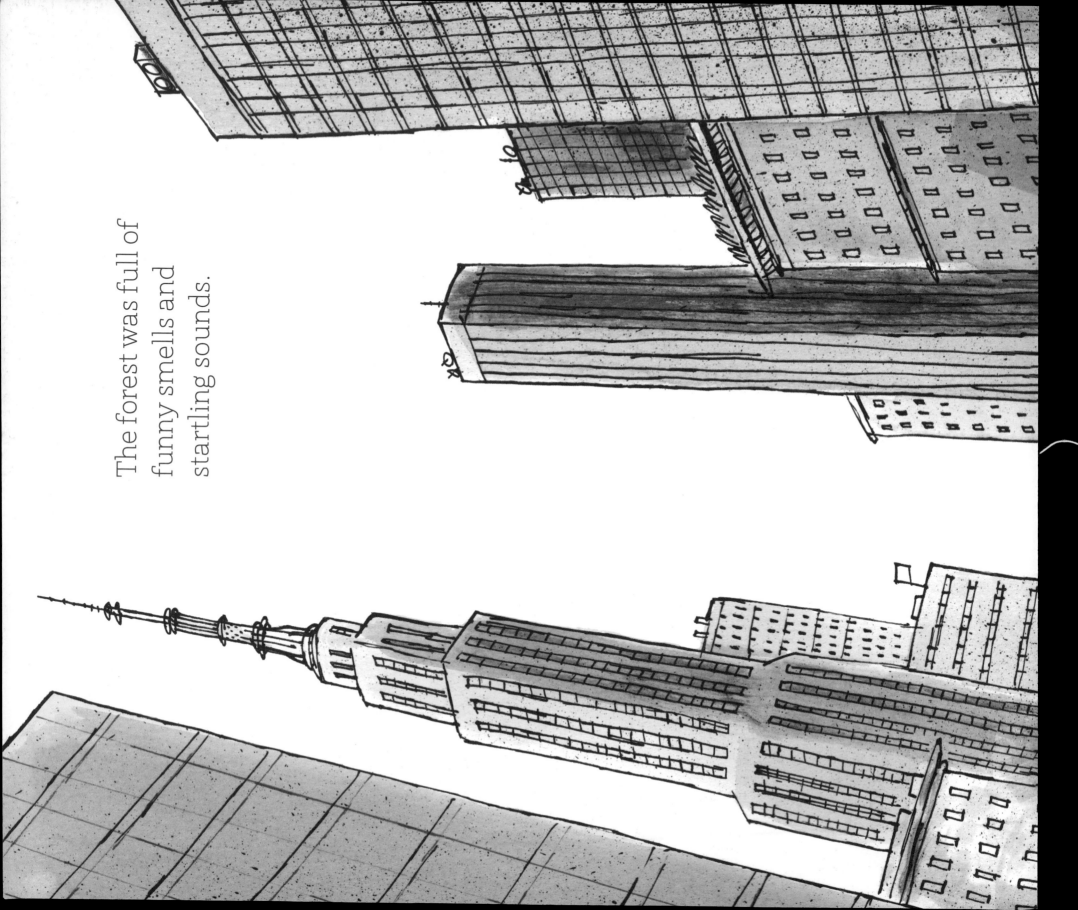

The forest was full of funny smells and startling sounds.

The mammoth found a good spot for breakfast . . .

and a lagoon for his bath.

The sun was warming his woolly back, and he began to feel a bit better.

But the cavemen gave him funny looks.
He wasn't sure why.
In fact, he wasn't sure about very much at all.

So he tried to make friends . . .

and to blend in.

He pretended to understand things
that he did not understand one bit.

But nobody understood him.

Ever.

He did his best to make himself useful,

but all he got were funny looks.
And sometimes angry shouting.

No herd.
Nobody to trumpet with.

It was all a bit much.

But wait. What was this?

The mammoth got himself all spruced up.
He bought his ticket, he stood in line
for hours and hours,

till eventually . . .

. . . there they were!

The mammoth trumpeted wildly!

But his herd did not trumpet back.
The mammoth took a closer look.

Hang on . . .

This was not his herd.
No. Definitely not his herd.

The mammoth was so disappointed
he went on a rampage.

Where were they?
Why did they leave him?
How did he end up in this stupid forest
where nobody understood him?

The mammoth had SO many questions.
But he didn't know who to ask,
nor who would understand.

Was he the only mammoth
in the world?

Then, above the din and the racket and the noisy beetles,
he heard a faint, faint trumpeting sound.

It was a strange sound. Not a mammoth sound.
But it was beautiful, and the mammoth understood it.

The mammoth listened for a long time,
thinking about his lost friends.

Then he lifted his trunk,
and began to trumpet along.

At first, his trumpeting sounded all wonky and wrong.

But as he started to get the hang of it,
his music grew stronger,

and louder,

and prouder . . .

... and the little cavepeople understood.

And they trumpeted and tootled
and honked and strummed,

till the moon shone high above.

Some people still give the mammoth funny looks.
And some still stamp and shout.

But who cares? Not the mammoth.

He has found his herd.
And a place to trumpet wildly.

For Aida,
Wren, Sylvia and Mateo
— A.K.

FOR MAX, SARAH,
WILSON AND BEAVIS — A.B.